Fairy Tale Theater
PUSS 'N BOOTS

Illustrations by: CARME PERIS
Adapted by: MÓNICA BOSOM

CHARACTERS:
Puss 'N Boots, the Marquis of Carabas, the King, Farmers, Countrymen, the Ogre, the Princess

Narrator:

There once was a miller who left his belongings to his three sons when he died. To the oldest, he left the mill, to the middle one, he left a donkey, and to the youngest, he left a cat, Puss.

Youngest Son:

"What a joke! My brothers will be able to make their living but I ... I will not be able to make a living with only a cat and I will starve."

Puss: *(It had heard everything.)*

"Do not worry, My lord. Give me a sack and some good boots and I will show you that what you have inherited will bring you wealth."

Youngest Son:

"What are you planning? Well, I have nothing to lose so I will give you a sack and some boots."

Narrator:

The cat puts on the red leather boots, takes the sack and some rope, and goes into the forest.

Puss 'N Boots:

"I will put a carrot and some cabbage leaves inside the sack. Then, maybe a careless little rabbit will fall into my trap."

Narrator:

Soon a little rabbit is caught in the cat's trap.

Puss 'N Boots:

"This is good luck! I will make this little rabbit my first present to our King."

Narrator:

Puss 'N Boots goes to the King's palace and decides to refer to his master as the Marquis of Carabas.

Puss 'N Boots:

"Your Majesty, please accept this rabbit that my lord, the Marquis of Carabas, humbly offers you."

King:

"Thank you. Tell your lord I am sincerely grateful."

Narrator:

For some months, Puss 'N Boots continues to take rabbits and partridges to the King on behalf of his master, the Marquis of Carabas.

Puss 'N Boots: *(To his master)*

"My lord, the King intends to ride along the river with his daughter. If you follow my advice, you will not be poor much longer. Take off your clothes and go swim in the river, exactly where I tell you. I will do the rest."

Marquis of Carabas:

"I do not understand, but I will do as you say."

Narrator:

While the Marquis of Carabas is swimming in the river, the King goes by in his coach.

Puss 'N Boots:

"Help, help! My master, the Marquis of Carabas, is drowning! Please, somebody help me!"

King: *(Recognizing the cat)*

"Guards, take the Marquis of Carabas out of the river before he drowns!"

Puss 'N Boots: *(Approaches the King and whispers)*

"Oh, my King! There is another problem. While the Marquis of Carabas was swimming in the river, a thief came and stole all his clothes. It would not be appropriate if the Princess saw him in this state."

King:

"Oh, that is no problem! Grooms, go get some appropriate clothes for the Marquis of Carabas and tell him to come into my coach. I want to meet this generous Marquis who has been sending me game to eat."

Narrator:

So the Marquis is dressed like a true Marquis and accompanies the King. His new clothes fit him so well that the Princess falls in love with him immediately.

(Meanwhile, Puss 'N Boots runs ahead of the coach and talks to some farmers who are working in the fields.)

Puss 'N Boots:

"My good people, please do me a favor and you will be fairly rewarded. When our King asks you who owns these fields, you have to answer that they belong to the Marquis of Carabas."

King:

"My good farmers, who owns these well-kept fields?"

Farmers:

"The Marquis of Carabas, Sire."

Puss 'N Boots: *(Once again ahead of the coach)*
"My good people, if you do not say these fields you are harvesting belong to the Marquis of Carabas, your happiness will soon be over."

King:
"My good countrymen, who owns these beautiful meadows?"

Countrymen:
"The Marquis of Carabas, Sire."

Narrator:
Puss 'N Boots says the same thing to all the people he meets on the way, and the King is more and more surprised and impressed by the possessions of the Marquis. Finally, Puss 'N Boots arrives at a castle that belongs to a wicked Ogre, as does all the land the King has been visiting.

Puss 'N Boots: *(Knocking at the castle door)*
Knock, knock, knock!

Ogre:

"Who are you? What do you want?"

Puss 'N Boots:

"Mister Ogre, your fame is so great that, as I was passing by, I thought it would be an honor for me to pay my respects to you."

Ogre: *(Surprised and pleased)*

"Oh, come in, come in and get some rest."

Puss 'N Boots:

"I have heard it said that you have the power to become whatever animal you want, for example a lion or an elephant."

Ogre:

"You can see it for yourself."
(The ogre turns himself into a lion.)

Puss 'N Boots: *(Frightened)*

"I must confess you have impressed me. But if your power is so great, could you also become a simple mouse?"

Ogre:

"Well, just look!"

Narrator:

As soon as the Ogre turns into a little mouse, Puss 'N Boots pounces on it and eats it up. Meanwhile, the King's coach has arrived in front of the castle and the cat comes out to meet him.

King: *(Addressing the Marquis of Carabas)*

"This lovely castle, is it yours too? I'd like to go inside and see it."

Puss 'N Boots:

"Your Majesty I welcome you to the castle of the Marquis of Carabas."

Marquis of Carabas: *(Taking the hand of the Princess and addressing the King)*

"Please go ahead, I will be honored if you are the first to go in."

Narrator:

They enter the beautiful castle and the King is very impressed. He thinks the Marquis of Carabas would be a good husband for his daughter and he says:

King:

"Marquis, Sir, would you be my son-in-law?"

Marquis of Carabas:

"Oh my King, Sire, it would be a great honor for me."

Narrator:

The Marquis and the Princess are married that same day, and Puss 'N Boots becomes a great gentleman and never again has to catch mice. Well, he sometimes does, but just for fun.

ACTIVITIES

Some of the activities related to this play can include:

1. Building the King's coach. You will need bottle corks, toothpicks, glue and paint. Use the glue and toothpicks to hold the corks together. Let the glue dry, and then paint your coach.

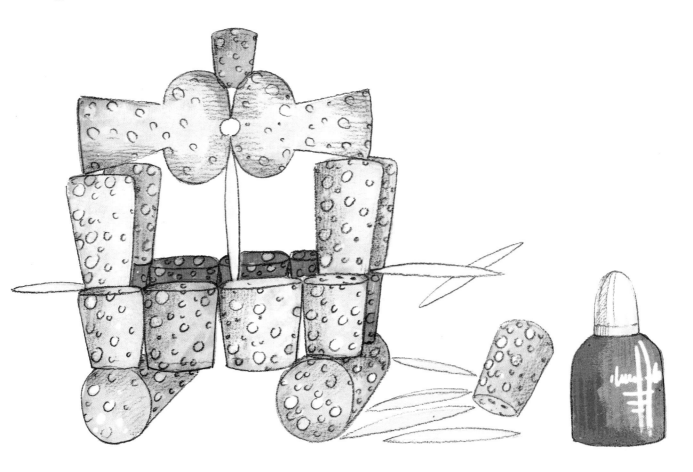

2. Make a puzzle with your own picture. You will need a large picture of each child, scissors, a pencil, cardboard, and glue.

Cut the cardboard to the same size as the picture. Glue the picture to the cardboard and then draw the lines of the puzzle on the back using a pencil. Cut the cardboard along the pencil lines and mix up the pieces. Children are now ready to put together a puzzle of their own picture.

3. Recipe for cheesecake

Ingredients:
4 packages of cream cheese—8 oz. (227 g) each
3 containers of plain yogurt—8 oz. (227 g) each
3 tablespoons (45 g) cornmeal
3 eggs
10 tablespoons (150 g) sugar
For the caramel:
3 tablespoons (45 ml) water
3 tablespoons (45 g) sugar

Pour the caramel ingredients into a mold and microwave on high for 6 minutes. Using oven mitts, take the mold out of the oven and tip it so that the caramel sticks to all sides. While the caramel sets, mix the remaining ingredients together until smooth. Pour the batter into the mold and microwave for 13 minutes. Let cool and then refrigerate. Serve cold.

4. Another activity consists of making very simple finger puppets. Cut out each character shown in the illustration and paste onto cardboard. Make the two cuts indicated in the drawing.

Place the puppets on your fingers and act out the story.

 --- cut

--- cut

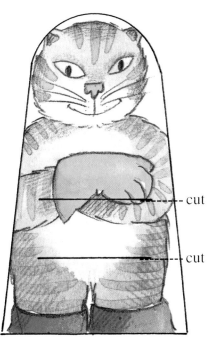 --- cut

--- cut

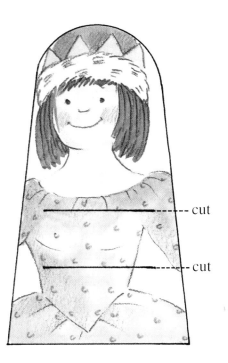 --- cut

--- cut

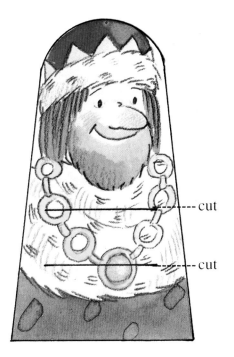 --- cut

--- cut

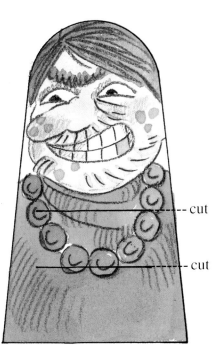 --- cut

--- cut

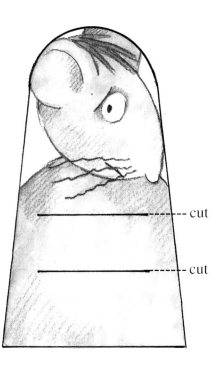 --- cut

--- cut

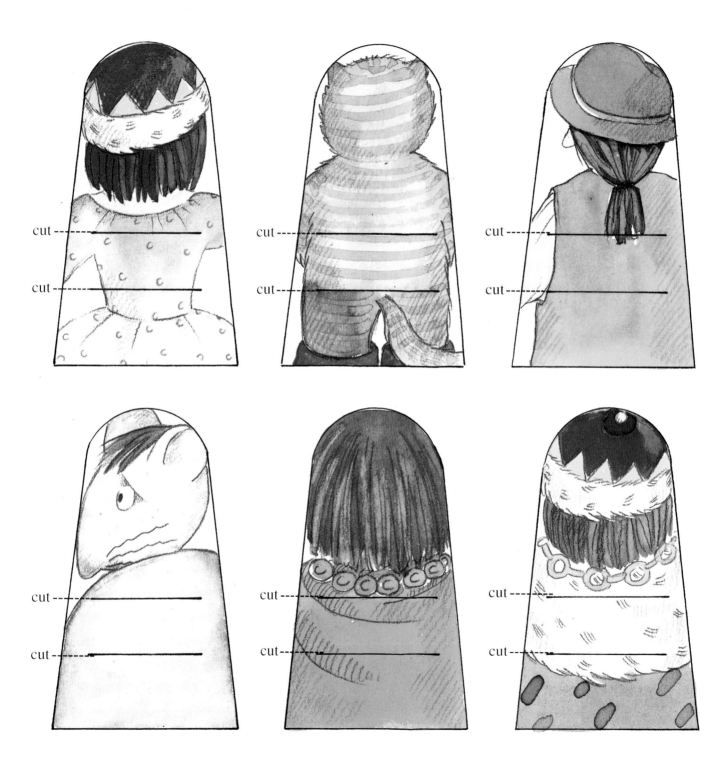

English language version published by Barron's Educational Series, Inc., 1999

Original title of the book in Catalan:
EL GAT AMB BOTES
One in the series *Teatre dels contes*
Illustrations by Carme Peris
Adapted by Mónica Bosom
Design by Carme Peris

All inquiries should be addressed to:
Barron's Educational Series, Inc.
250 Wireless Boulevard
Hauppauge, New York 11788
http://www.barronseduc.com

International Standard Book No. 0-7641-5156-8

Library of Congress Catalog Card No. 98-73635

Printed in Spain
9 8 7 6 5 4 3 2 1